For a sardine, there's nothing more important than safety, believe me.

To Deirdre and Saho

About This Book

The illustrations for this book were created using scanned mixed media and Kyle T. Webster brushes in Photoshop. This book was edited by Deirdre Jones and designed by Angelie Yap under the art direction of Saho Fujii. The production was supervised by Lillian Sun, and the production editor was Annie McDonnell. The text was set in Smug Seagull, and the display type is hand-lettered.

JUST BE JELLY

maddie frost

LB

Little, Brown and Company

New York Boston

We have 19,000 rules in the sardine safety handbook.
And the number one rule is STICK TOGETHER.

The ocean is FULL of dangerous species.

Swimming in a group is much safer than swimming alone.

There could be ANYTHING around the next reef.

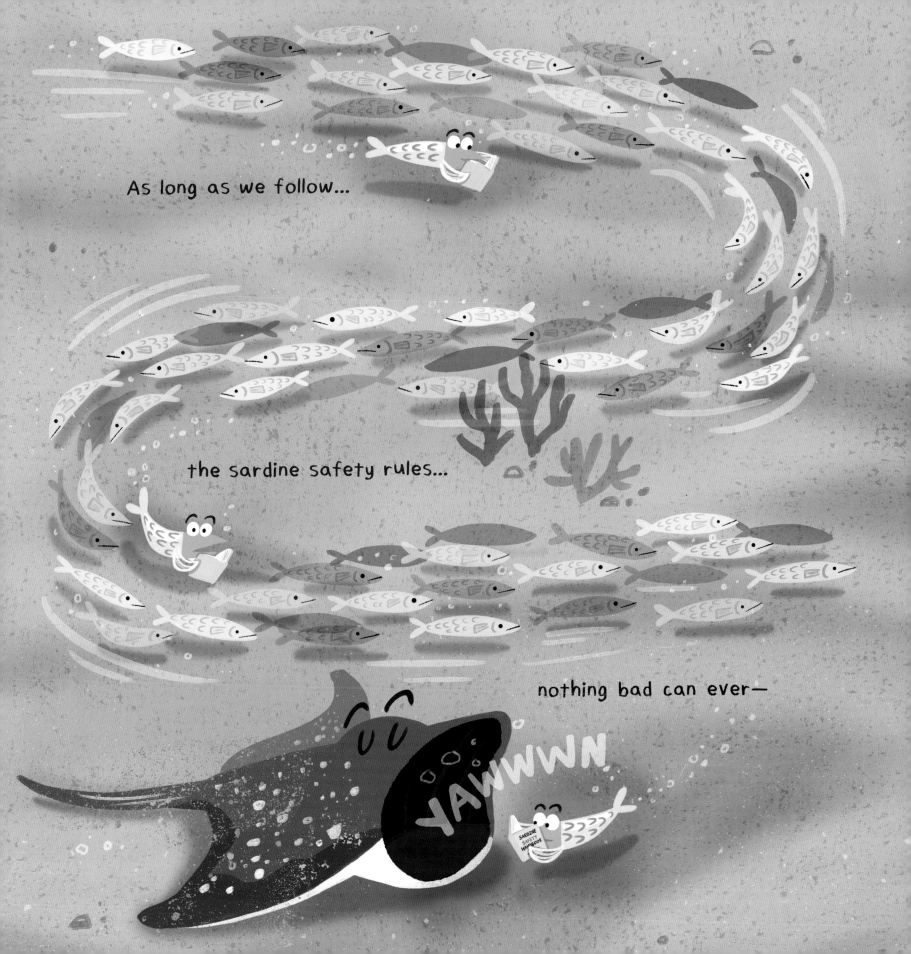

Oh thank goodness! I almost lost you guys!

See what happens when you don't follow the—

Wait a minute. This is not my group.

OH. MY. COD.
THIS IS NOT MY GROUP!

Sardine safety rule number 2,455:
If you lose your group, STAY CALM.
They are never far away!

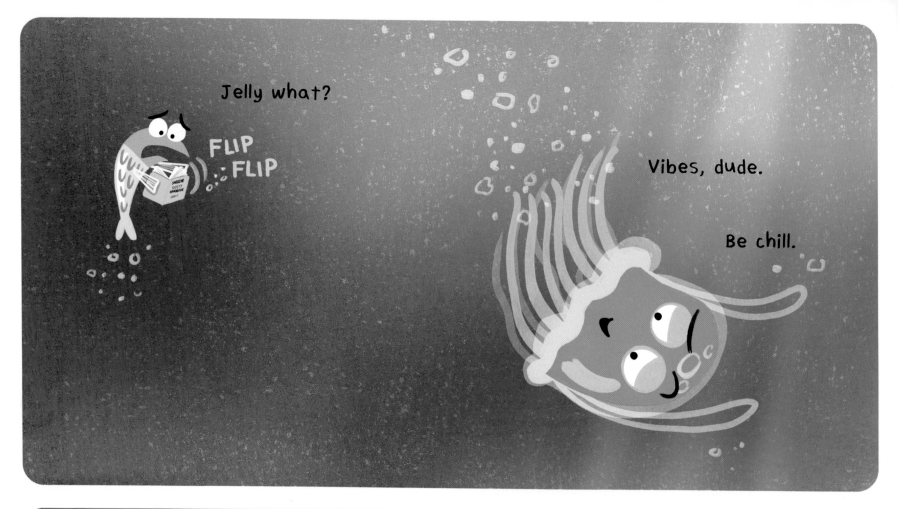

Wiggle up.

Wiggle down.

Wiggle all around.

Now go with the flow.

And just be jelly. You dig?

No, I do not DIG. Do you really think being JELLY will save me from a hungry predator?

The predator will say, "You look like a tasty snack!"

And I'll say, "Joke's on you, predator. I've got jelly vibes to save me!"

Then it'll EAT ME.

I prefer to stick to the rules! But thanks anyway, jellyfish.

Um...

RAWR!

BOOGA-BOOGA!

I have a clam and I'm not afraid to use it!

Please put me down.

Okay, that's it!
BACK OFF, PREDATORS!
I've got JELLY VIBES!

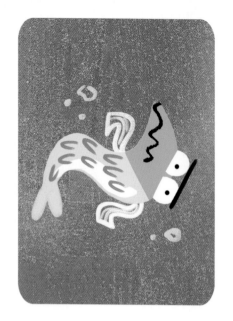

Now I feel better... but I still can't find my group.

Hey, I think I saw a group of sardines.

They swam this way.

Let's make new rules!

WHOOSH

Slow down.

Get distracted.

Be friendly.

And...